This book belongs to

....

D0493330

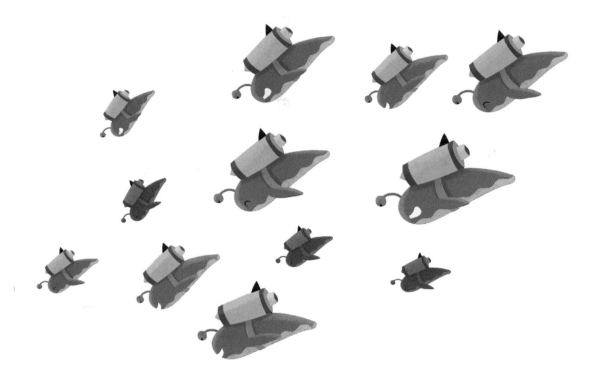

Quarto is the authority on a wide range of topics.

Quarto educates, entertains and enriches the lives of our readers—enthusiasts and lovers of hands-on living.

www.quartoknows.com

© 2019 Quarto Publishing plc

First published in 2019 by QED Publishing, an imprint of The Quarto Group. The Old Brewery, 6 Blundell Street, London N7 9BH, United Kingdom. T (0)20 7700 6700 F (0)20 7700 8066 www.QuartoKnows.com

A catalogue record for this book is available from the British Library.

ISBN 978-0-71124-385-9

Based on the original story by Peter Bently and Duncan Beedie

Author of adapted text: Katie Woolley
Series Editor: Joyce Bentley
Series Designer: Sarah Peden

Manufactured in Shenzhen, China PP052019

9 8 7 6 5 4 3 2 1

Reading Gems

Mr Whimple's Potion

Focus sounds in this book

ay (ai)
d**ay**

ou (ow)
h**ou**se

ou (oo short)
c**ou**ld

ie (igh)
fl**ie**s

ea (ee)
m**ea**n

oy (oi)
t**oy**

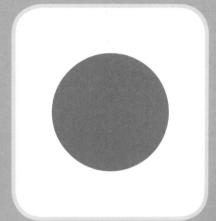

ir (er)
thi**r**sty

ue (oo long)
bl**ue**

aw (or)
s**aw**

ew (oo long)
n**ew**

wh (w)
Whimple

Ready?
Let's Go!

5

The bugs.

I am Nid.

I am San.

I am Gop.

I am Pem.

One day, the bugs saw a ship in the sky. It was heading for Planet Bug.

Crash!

There were lots of blue bottles in the ship.

"Oh, it looks like milk!' said Nid.

He took a big gulp!

The drink was not milk.
Yuck!

The bugs tried to find where the ship came from.

"Here is a sign," said San.

Planet
Poob

The bugs wanted to fly
off to Planet Poob.

"Where is Nid?"
asked Pem.

The bugs looked in Nid's house.

They looked out and about.

"He must be having a nap," said Gop.

Gop, San and Pem went to Planet Poob.

By the time they got there,
San was very hungry.

She could not see her lunch box.

"A castle!" said Gop. "I'm sure they will have some food."

15

The castle was old Mr Whimple's house.

"The slugs want to smash
my house!" he called.

Mr Whimple had made a potion to stop them.

It was in his ship but the ship had gone.

"We can help you," said the bugs.
"Your potion is on Planet Bug."

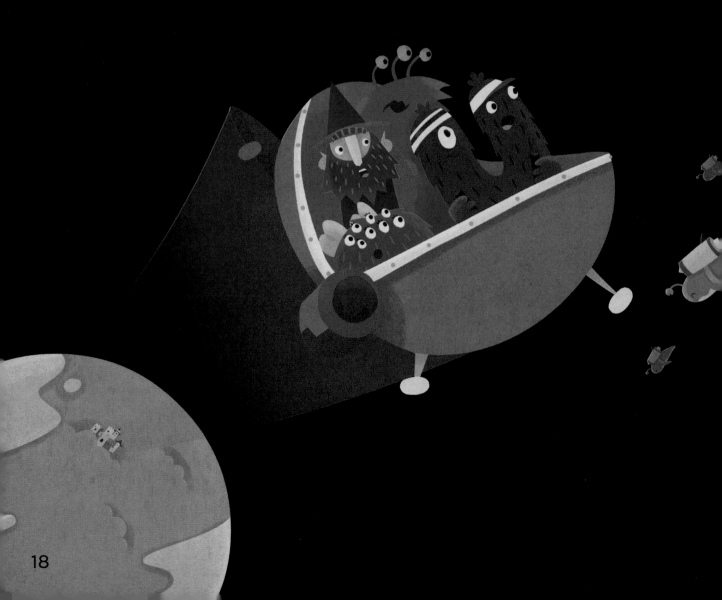

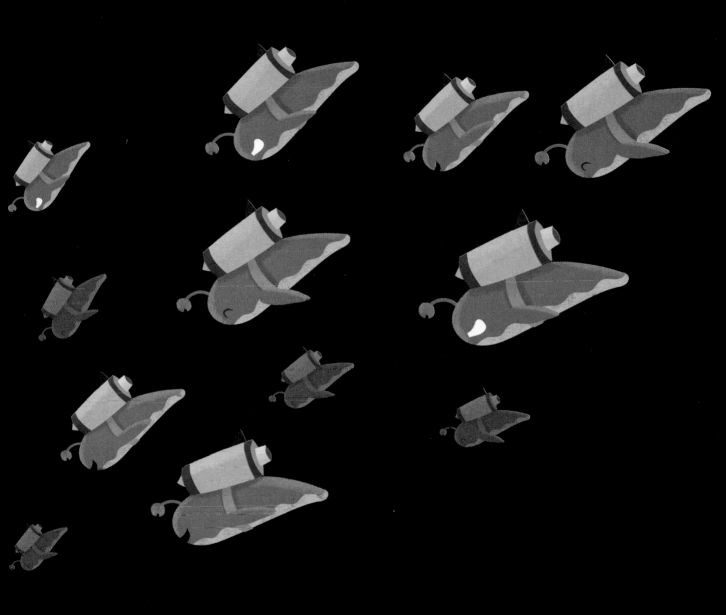

The bugs saw the slugs.

"They look mean," said Pem.

19

The bugs put the blue bottles in the ship.

San even saw her lunch box.

The bugs zoomed back to Planet Poob.

The swarm of slugs landed.

"I'm thirsty," said the chief slug.
"I need a drink."

The slugs drank the potion.
They turned into little toy flies!

San opened her lunch box.
"Here is little Nid!" she said.

Old Mr Whimple gave Nid a new potion.
He was big again. Phew!

25

Let's Talk About Mr Whimple's Potion

Look at the front cover.

What sound do you think Mr Whimple is making here?

Can you write down the sound?

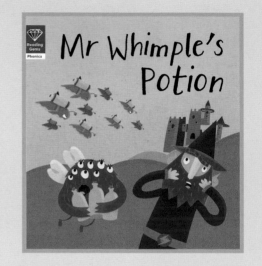

This story focuses on different letter patterns for the same sound.

Can you read these words from the story?

day milk fly old new potion chief

Find the letter pattern 'Wh' at the beginning of the old man's name. What sound does it make?

Can you sound out the whole name?

Why was Mr Whimple sad?

How did the bugs save the day?

What did the bugs do at the end of the story?

Did you like the story about old Mr Whimple's potion?

What was your favourite bit?

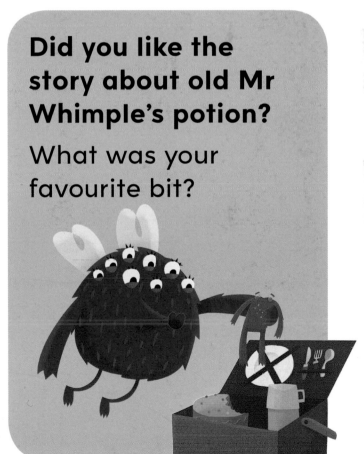

27

Fun and Games

Different spellings can make the same sound.

Choose the letters to spell the words.

1

or

ar   or

sw .... m

2

ur

ir   er

th .... sty

3

sh

s   t

po .... ion

28

4

w

wh   w

.... imple

5

ow

ough ou

h .... se

6

oo (long)

oo ue

bl .... bottles

Reading With Your Little Bugs

Here are some tips to help you enjoy reading this book with your child.

1 Encourage your child to read the story to you, saying the sounds and putting them together to read the word.

2 If your child gets stuck on a word, show them how to break it down into sounds.

3 Have fun! You could make up silly voices for each of the characters and even act out the story together.

4 Remember to give your child lots of praise!

5 If your child is starting to feel tired or bored, put the book away and pick it up another day.

Have fun and enjoy reading my story together.

Mind-Boggling Phonics Glossary

Phonics often feels a bit confusing,
with lots of alien terms. This glossary
will help demystify Phonics!

blend to put individual sounds together to read a word, e.g. s-n-a-p blended together reads 'snap'.

CVC word a word spelled with a consonant, then a vowel, then a consonant, like 'sat' or 'tip'.

decode to put sounds and letters together to read a word correctly.

digraph two letters representing one sound, e.g. ck in 'kick'.

grapheme a letter or group of letters representing one sound, e.g. t, b, sh, ch, igh, ough (as in 'though').

phoneme a single unit of sound, e.g. the letter 't' represents just one sound and the letters 'sh' represent just one sound.

segment to split up a word into its individual phonemes in order to spell, e.g. the word 'cat' has three phonemes: /c/ /a/ /t/.

sight words or high-frequency words are words that appear most often in printed materials. They may not be decodable using phonics (or too advanced) but they are useful to learn separately by sight to develop fluency in reading.

tricky words are words that cannot be sounded out with phonics, such as 'the', 'was' and 'one'. Sometimes called exception words.

trigraph three letters representing one sound, e.g. igh in 'night'.

31

GET TO KNOW READING GEMS

Reading Gems is a series of books that has been written for children who are learning to read. The books have been created in consultation with a literacy specialist.

The books fit into five levels, with each level getting more challenging as a child's confidence and reading ability grows. The simple text and fun illustrations provide gradual, structured practice of reading. Most importantly, these books are good stories that are fun to read!

Phonics is for children who are learning their letters and sounds. Simple, engaging stories provide gentle phonics practice.

Level 1 is for children who are taking their first steps into reading. Story themes and subjects are familiar to young children, and there is lots of repetition to build reading confidence.

Level 2 is for children who have taken their first reading steps and are becoming readers. Story themes are still familiar but sentences are a bit longer, as children begin to tackle more challenging vocabulary.

Level 3 is for children who are developing as readers. Stories and subjects are varied, and more descriptive words are introduced.

Level 4 is for readers who are rapidly growing in reading confidence and independence. There is less repetition on the page, broader themes are explored and plot lines straddle multiple pages.

Phonics

There were lots of blue bottles in the ship.
"Oh, it looks like milk!' said Nid.

He took a big gulp!

The drink was not milk. Yuck!

Simple sentences ✓

Specific sounds and letters ✓

Repeated tricky words ✓

Pictures and words support one another ✓